Danielle

A Bliss Bay Romance
Kayla Love

Corner of Press

ISBN-13: 979-8-9874241-6-2

Cover Design by: Corner of Press

Artwork by: Nadezhda

Chapter 1
Stuck

How did I get here? Danielle wondered, metaphorically, as she looked out of the cab window and up at the Empire State Building lit up in purple. In an alternate universe, Danielle was curled up on the couch watching a scary movie with Marcus. In reality, she'd hopped on Amtrak on a whim to come to her best friend Brandy's 'Boos & Booze Halloween Party' - the first event Brandy and her new boo, Jalen, were hosting together at his place in Brooklyn. After seeing how truly happy and cherished Brandy was in this new relationship, Danielle realized something was missing in hers. If you could call it that. It was definitely more of a situationship than a relationship for starters.

Marcus had been her on-again, off-again, friend with benefits for the past six years. But six hours ago, Danielle decided enough was enough and cut things off. Ultimately, she knew she deserved better than accepting the crumbs she'd been letting herself settle for. Eventually. She needed a break first. She decided to swear off men until at least the new year! But in the meantime, she needed a distraction. She called Brandy.

"Hey B?" she asked.

"Hey D. What's up?" Danielle could hear the sounds of a bustling bodega in the background. Brandy must have been doing last minute shopping for the party.

"Well, actually. I was wondering if you had room for one more at this party later. I cut things off with Marcus and need a distraction."

"For real?! Damn, D. That's a big deal. But I'm not surprised. You deserved better. You okay?"

"Yeah. I know. And I will be."

"Aww. Yeah! Come on up! And plenty of J's friends will be here, so maybe there will be a love connection. Heyyyy!" Brandy exclaimed.

Danielle smiled. Brandy was love struck! She was normally much more pragmatic than romantic, but Jalen had her spellbound. And planning on matching costumes. As Beyonce and Jay-Z, of course!

And so here she was. In a cab. On the way to a party of mostly strangers. Regretting her hasty choice to put on this sexy cat costume under her trench coat. It was uncomfortable trying to sit with this damn tail! She knew the party would have started by the time she arrived, so she decided to save time and just wear the costume.

A few minutes later she was buzzing to be let into the party. As she walked through the door she heard, "Can you hold the door, please?" from a deep voice behind her.

"Thanks!" the voice said as he walked in behind her. "You headed to the party, too?"

"Yeah," she said, as she finally took a good look at the guy. He had a fake black eye and a black shirt with a 'P' on it. "Wait. Are you a black-eyed pea?"

"Yup!" he replied, looking proud. "You are ....Inspector Gadget?" he asked as they began walking up the stairs.

She chuckled at his corniness. But she did kind of look like Inspector Gadget with this trench. "Nope. A cat," she explained as she opened up the coat and revealed her leopard print leotard. "It was last minute."

"No. It looks good," he replied as they approached the door. Danielle, in her "I'm over men" state, completely missed how this guy's eyes went wide at the sight of her tiny waist and toned legs. "I'm Andrew, by the way." He held out a hand.

"Danielle," she replied, shaking it back.

The moment was interrupted by the door to Jalen's apartment opening and the sounds of "Thriller" greeting them. They disappeared into the party. Andrew migrated toward the bar set up in the kitchen and Danielle made a beeline for Brandy.

The party was bustling. The music was bumping, the drinks were flowing, and a constant stream of people were in and out, mixing and mingling. Danielle did her best to interact despite knowing so few people and truly hating small talk. But it did give her something to do to keep her mind off Marcus and to give Brandy some room to host without her being glued to her side the entire night.

Like she often did when she was in situations where she felt awkward or out of place, she made it a game in her head. She would challenge her inner Oprah. *Okay. What can I learn besides somebody's job? How many people can I get to give me a real story?*

By the end of the night, she'd collected a few. She learned about one woman's out of body experience at the Running of the Bulls after asking about her all white attire accented by a red sash and scarf. She'd added a few books to her GoodReads list after a conversation with a guy dressed like "pumpkin pi" who was a Ph.D. student in history. She even got the juicy news that one of the women was knocked up! Danielle was minding her business pouring some bourbon into a red cup when she noticed the woman pouring her beer out of the bottle and into a cup and then replacing the contents with seltzer.

"Does that beer suck that bad?" Danielle joked.

The woman got wide eyed and looked over her shoulder before whispering, "Shhh. Not everyone knows yet, but I'm pregnant!"

"Congratulations!" Danielle whispered back. "Our secret."

She was happy to pass some of the time chatting with Brandy's older cousin, Gabby and her boyfriend, Dev, who were dressed like Catwoman and Batman. She and Brandy always thought Gabby's life was #goals. She was a successful entertainment lawyer, with a badass apartment, epic shoe collection, and hot boyfriend. A romantic at heart, Gabby always believed in happily ever afters. She left Danielle with some parting words about true love being right around the corner. Danielle sure hoped it would be.

Before long, most of the guests were trickling out of the party onto the streets of Brooklyn. Brandy was staying at Jalen's for the night. She offered Danielle a spot on his couch, but Danielle opted to take her best friend's keys and crash up at Brandy's place.

"I will be back in the morning and we can chat over brunch, okay, D?" Brandy said, taking Danielle's hand in hers.

"Sounds good, B. Love you!" she said, giving Brandy a big hug.

"Don't forget to text me when you get in!" Brandy shouted after her.

In the entryway of Jalen's building, Danielle waited on her Uber. *Really? It said 3 minutes 5 minutes ago!* She impatiently waited. She couldn't wait to get out of these boots. While she was waiting, Andrew came down the steps shortly after.

"Damn," she overheard him mutter. "22 minutes!"

"Uber times?" she asked. "Yeah. Mine was supposed to be here in 3 minutes," she said using air quotes. "But here we are 7 minutes later."

"You live nearby?" he asked.

"No, actually. I live in Baltimore. I'm just heading uptown to Brandy's to stay the night."

"Oh okay. Yeah, Brandy's cool. I met her at the beach last summer. I'm not sure if you know Jeremy from the house, but he's a buddy of mine."

Danielle looked down at her app. The Uber driver canceled.

"For real!" she muttered. "My Uber canceled. Guess I am staying here after all."

"Where are you headed?" Andrew asked.

"Upper West," Danielle informed him.

"Why don't you hop in with me? If you don't mind waiting..." he looked down at his phone. "Seven minutes. I can add a stop."

"Don't go out of your way. It's really fine."

"It's really no bother."

"Okay, thanks."

Danielle was tired and not thrilled about having to keep making small talk with this guy, but she did want to get to Brandy's. He was nice enough, but she was emotionally zapped.

"You been out to Bliss Bay at all?" Andrew asked.

"I haven't actually. Brandy talks about how great it is all the time though. I need to," Danielle responded.

She did really need to though. She'd hesitated because, honestly, even though Brandy was her best friend in the whole world, they had some differences in their upbringings and friend groups. Brandy grew up in a middle class, suburban New Jersey town and had spent a lot of time with her white friends and in white spaces. Danielle grew up in a working class Maryland town surrounded mostly by other

Black folks. She knew Brandy's Bliss Bay crew was mostly white, but hey. She somehow met Jalen out there so maybe Danielle could be a bit more open.

"Finally! Uber's here," Andrew stated. Danielle followed him out and into the car. When they were in the car, he asked, "So, Danielle, where does your costume rank in your all time top Halloween costumes?"

Well, that was better than the usual, 'What do you do for work?' questions most folks ask. "Eh. Middle of the road. I came up here last minute and it was the first thing I could find. I think the all time best was when Brandy and I were Salt-n-Pepa in college!"

"That's a good one. The important question though...did you have a Spinderella?" he asked.

Danielle was caught off guard for a beat. What did this seemingly basic white boy know about Spinderella?

"We did not."

"Ok, ok."

"What about you? Is this your best costume?"

"Nah. I think Clark Kent was the best. I mean, maybe a little too on the nose since I'm a journalist," Andrew said.

"Oh really. What type?" Danielle inquired.

"Economics reporter. Trust me. It's more exciting than it sounds."

"Oh I know. I'm in journalism, too. Content Editor for my local NPR."

"Nice! What made you choose radio?"

Before Danielle could answer, the car came to a halt on the Manhattan Bridge.

"Looks like an accident. GPS is saying at least 30 minutes until we get off the bridge," the driver said.

Danielle let out a sigh. Andrew was a little corny, but a good conversationalist, so Danielle didn't mind talking, but she also was exhausted and had only mentally prepared to keep up a conversation for a short time. She looked down at her phone hoping that she could amuse herself a bit with a game or scrolling social media as the conversation lulled.

Ugh. 12%.

And, of course, in the rush she didn't put her backup charger in her bag. And this wasn't one of those fancy Ubers with chargers. Looks like she was going to have to keep chatting with this Andrew guy after all....

Chapter 2
Unsatisfied

A little after 3 a.m., Danielle finally found herself safe and cozy in Brandy's apartment. She removed her boots from her feet in the doorway.

"Ahhh." She exhaled audibly. She removed the rest of her costume and headed to the shower. The hot water felt nice after the bit of chill in the air. Hot tears commingled with the drops of warm water from the shower head as she finally allowed herself to process the past 18 hours.

Her situationship with Marcus had been gnawing at her for the past few months. What once was a source of comfort and consistency and fun had started feeling less fulfilling, like Chinese food after a hangover. Hits the spot in the moment, but leaves you wanting something more shortly after. Yes, they enjoyed each other's company. They had similar taste in movies and could hold decent conversations. And he always made sure she was satisfied first. But Danielle wanted more than casual conversations and occasional orgasms. She wanted to be truly seen. Even though that was scary AF. Clearly. She'd been okay avoiding it up until now. And even though it was her choice, it still hurt like hell.

In the early days, they at least faked the funk a bit. They'd schedule times to see each other, put a little effort into the snacks, watch something on the steamier side to get in the mood. But this Friday, like many of the past few, Marcus had sent a text earlier that day and Danielle agreed to him coming over.

She had some popcorn and half a bottle of wine she'd open the night before. They watched Dateline, then, like clockwork, moved into her bedroom where they went through the motions of him stripping down to his boxers and her changing into an oversized t-shirt that would end up on the floor soon enough anyway.

They crawled into her bed and under the sheets where within mere moments she could feel the warmth of Marcus's chest, and hardness, against her back. His hand moved her locs off her shoulder and then found its way around her body to massage her breasts. Her body responded in turn as she arched her back and pressed her ass against him. His hand moved further south and his fingers found the precise spot between her thighs he knew would drive her over the edge, gently strumming her like a guitar. Her body writhed with pleasure and her breath quickened at his touch. She rolled onto her back so that Marcus could find his way on top of her. She grabbed at the waistband of his boxer briefs and pulled them down to his knees as she pleaded for his entry. From there, Marcus pulled them the rest of the way off and found his way inside of her. She could only prolong her pleasure for so long before she collapsed in a heap on the bed.

After catching her breath, she got up to use the bathroom and brush her teeth. Back in her room, she put on her t-shirt and crawled under the covers where Marcus joined after his trip to the bathroom. Per usual, he was on the other side of the bed. She knew by now in their situation that cuddling didn't mean anything, but given how far Marcus always stayed on the other side of the bed, she wasn't convinced he was of the same school of thought.

The next morning, Marcus left shortly after the sun rose. At that moment, something inside her felt empty. Usually a session at the gym alleviated those feelings, so she went and got in a workout, but this time she couldn't shake it. So after, she gave him a call from her car and asked if he could meet up. He couldn't, so she just blurted out that this wasn't working for her anymore. He simply said he understood. After they hung up, she let a few thug tears escape. She wasn't a crier, but clearly this had been weighing on her. And maybe there was a little bit of ego and pride wrapped up in it, too. *Why wasn't he more upset?*

She still wondered as she turned off the shower. She wouldn't solve her relationship problems right now so it was best to get some rest. She dried off and pulled some PJs out of Brandy's bottom drawer and climbed into the bed. She sent a quick text to Brandy and then was sound asleep as soon as her head hit the pillow.

The next morning, Danielle was awoken by the sound of keys jingling in the door. Must be Brandy. Danielle had taken Brandy's keys so she assumed she was using a spare set she'd given to Jalen. She felt a slight pang in her heart, which she knew was her longing to be in a relationship with a man she could give a set of keys to.

She then heard Brandy's footsteps walking to the bathroom and then the sounds of the shower running. She dozed off and was awakened a few minutes later by Brandy, in her bathrobe, plopping next to her on the bed.

"Hey, D," Brandy said softly as she lightly rubbed Danielle's arm. "How ya feeling?"

Danielle's eyes opened and she looked into the freshly washed face of her best friend like she had many times before. There had been countless times the two of them laid up in one of their beds watching a movie, debriefing a night out, laughing, crying. Despite still being all up in her feelings, it did give her some comfort. She brushed her locs out of her face. "Hanging in..." she trailed off.

"Yeah..." Brandy replied, giving Danielle's arm a gentle squeeze. "Boozy brunch?"

"Yassss!" Danielle said as she sat up. "Mimosa me!"

A short while later, the best friends were seated across from each other with assorted beverages and a bread basket in front of them.

"Okay. Spill it." Brandy stated. "What's really going on, D?"

Danielle took a big sip of her jasmine tea before preparing to spill the tea. "Well," she started. "It just wasn't enough for me anymore. I realized I was tired of just settling for my situation with Marcus. He's a good dude. Don't get me wrong. But we ain't gettin' no younger. I really do want to find someone, get married, have some babies. For so long I was avoiding it. I mean, after the Kenan shit show and then Isaiah..."

Kenan was Danielle's ex from college. He was the backup center for the basketball team and a grade ahead. She met him at the tutoring center where she worked part time to pay for college. All the athletes were required to do office hours there and it was impossible not to notice him. She never thought he would be checking for her, but she had a feeling when she noticed he was coming on days he wasn't even scheduled and making it a point to connect with her. Before long, he asked her out and they started dating.

He was her first just about everything. Naively, she thought they would get married after college. She thought he was different from the stereotypical college athlete who screwed around. But, after two years, right before Kenan's graduation, she found out she was dead wrong and he was cheating with a girl at a rival college. She was crushed and vowed never to let a guy get that close to her heart again. That was until two years out of college.

She met Isaiah at a bar. Also a former college athlete. DIII Football. Now working as an accountant. She figured he may have gotten the cheating thing out of his system. It was true. He had. They had a nice thing going until Danielle got a promotion at work and was making more money than him. A traditionalist, his ego just couldn't handle it - or her ambitions. And so they parted ways.

Danielle went back to her comfort zone of short trysts. That is, until she met Marcus on a boat cruise she randomly went on when one of her college friends was in town. By the end of the night, they exchanged numbers and by the end of the month, they were seeing each other consistently. Initially, she thought maybe it would turn into something more, but when he never initiated anything beyond their arrangement, she resigned to being satisfied with a friends with benefits relationship.

"You know I'd never really seen a successful and happy Black couple until I met your parents, B?"

Brandy's parents reminded Danielle of the Huxtables. Happily married and supportive of each others careers. Whereas a number of Danielle's friends growing up had single moms and the ones that had partnered parents seemed to be in tumultuous relationships. Meanwhile, Danielle's parents had been high school sweethearts. They had never married and broke off their relationship when she was 7. They managed to amicably co-parent her, but her mom never dated. At least not to Danielle's knowledge. Her only real relationship advice to Danielle before college was "Focus on your grades and don't get pregnant. Save those boys for later!" Her dad, on the other hand, had only had a string of short term relationships. At least that she knew about. So she didn't have much to go on. Which is why she went into the Kenan situation rather naive. So after all of that, it was no wonder she put commitment on a shelf. But maybe it was time to consider something else.

She continued. "And now...seeing you with Jalen. We've been talking about it in therapy a lot and I'm realizing it could be possible for me, too."

"Of course it could! My best friend is a catch, okay! I mean, I know it ain't easy out in these dating streets. You know what my situation was like before Jalen. A hot ass mess. But it is possible, D."

"Yeah. But I need to cleanse my aura of the remnants of the old energy first!" Danielle gestured as if she was waving sage in front of herself. "Because as I learned, I was picking emotionally unavailable guys because I am also emotionally unavailable. Unpack that!" Danielle gestured a mic drop.

Brandy giggled and shook her head. "Girl. You will get there. For now, let's eat.

Chapter 3
Again

After they paid their check, the friends decided to walk a bit and burn off some of the food they ate.

"I have the perfect spot to take you!" Brandy exclaimed. They ambled along until they arrived at a shop selling old vinyls.

"Yooo! This store is dope!"

"I knew you'd love it."

Danielle was big into music. Her dad's influence. Some of her favorite memories from childhood were listening to vinyls on her dad's record player. As they perused the aisles, holding up various records from their favorite artists, Brandy asked, "Did you really not get in until 3?"

"Oh yeah....the Uber took a while and then there was traffic on the bridge. Ridiculous! Oh and my phone was almost dead so I had to small talk."

"Oh nooo. With the driver?" Brandy asked.

"Oh. No. With Andrew. He said he met you before. He's friends with one of the beach house guys."

"Oh yeah. Andrew! He's sweet. I don't know him well, but he seems like a good guy. How was it?"

"Not bad actually. He's actually pretty interesting. He's also a journalist. But what really got me was when I was telling him about the Halloween we were Salt n' Pepa and how he knew about Spinderella! I was like, this dude?!" Danielle chuckled.

"Well okay, Andrew! I guess it's a good reminder that people can be surprising. That whole not judging an album by its cover or whatever they say."

"Yeah...something like that."

A few hours later, Danielle was heading to the train back to Baltimore. Even that short time with her best friend was therapeutic. As the train pulled out of the station, she thought about what Brandy said. That people can be surprising. And not what meets the eye. Maybe that had been part of her problem, too. After she broke up with Isaiah, she really did cut herself off from anything meaningful and her criteria was exclusively how fun and how fine the guy was. I mean, she didn't need much more than that if she wasn't going to be serious with them. It was hard for her to imagine another way. Even though she knew she had to make some changes, she just couldn't imagine how that would play out.

Will I have to date a cornball?

She thought of some of the cornier guys she knew. How would she get through a first date with someone like that, let alone to a kiss, or anything more? She couldn't imagine that type being able to fulfill her bedroom needs. But maybe she'd be surprised.

Back in Baltimore, Danielle had a busy week at work so she didn't have time to think about what had happened with Marcus, getting back

out there, or anything else. But that was interrupted on Friday night.

After work, she stopped by her local wine shop to grab a bottle to take home to have with her take out. She was mostly a rum girl, but Brandy had introduced her to the world of wine and she enjoyed a good glass or two. Especially for a low key night at home. She was in the reds aisle looking for something to go with the pizza she was planning to order when she heard a familiar voice. Her heart felt like it was jumping out of her chest. That was definitely Marcus. *Shit!* She wasn't in the mood for a run in. *What is he even doing here? In my wine shop?* This was her neighborhood. Shouldn't it be her territory? Then she heard the distinct voice of a woman. *Great!* Even though it was her choice to move on, it still stung hearing him out with another woman already.

"We should get a moscato!" the woman exclaimed from the aisle over.

Danielle rolled her eyes and stifled a giggle. *Amateur hour...* She grabbed a bottle of Chianti and made her way toward checkout. She was going to try to get out of here unscathed but was prepared for the run if it happened. Luckily, she was able to pay and leave while the mystery woman and Marcus peered at labels of Moscato.

Back at home with her slice of pizza and hearty pour of wine, Danielle turned on the TV. She flipped through the new releases. She realized she didn't have the attention span for anything new, so she put on one of her comfort shows, *Girlfriends*. Two episodes, two slices, and a second glass of wine later, Danielle opened up her phone to Link, the newest dating app everyone was supposedly on. *No time like the present!* Even though she had initially sworn off dating until the new year, after her chat with Brandy she thought she might as well give it a dabble. It was this, or get out of her cozy clothes and hit up a local bar. She opted for this. For tonight.

She started answering the various questions. Name, height, education. Those were easy. Photos. Hmm. She probably needed a couple new ones, but she could make do with what she had. Then the more challenging part. The questions. *What's my mantra? What kind of question is that? Umm...fuck around and find out?* She let out a giggle. That probably wouldn't get her the outcome she wanted here. Maybe a different prompt. *Two truths and a lie?* That she could do. She's done it plenty of times for work. She started typing:

I interviewed Oprah (truth). In fact, it was the highlight of her career. She'd been chosen through an emerging leaders in journalism competition. *I speak fluent Spanish (truth).* Danielle grew up speaking with her Panamanian grandmother and then excelled at it in school. *I play piano (lie).* Although she loved music, she didn't play any instruments.

Now came the toughest part. Preferences. Now typically Danielle would easily check Black, 6' and above, post grad education, 32-38. But she thought about this idea of being more open. *But how open was too open?* Maybe she could get over if he was 30 or if he was 5'11. After all she was 5'6. But could she do a 40 year old, high school educated only man? Or a regular schmegular, 5'7 white man? She couldn't see it, but decided she would stay curious and let herself be surprised. But not too surprised. She chose all races, 5'9 and above, undergraduate education, and 30-40. That was growth. She decided she would save swiping for tomorrow. For now, it was time for a quick session with her vibrator and some sleep.

The next day, Danielle woke up parched. After setting up her profile, she had another hearty glass of wine. She promptly guzzled a large glass of water and then changed into her work-out clothes, sneakers, and a baseball cap to hit the gym. Not without a swipe of lip gloss though. In case of any run ins.

But there was no run in. She didn't even see any man worth checking out in the gourmet grocery store or her favorite bookstore, Charm City Books. She'd have to take her chances online. When she got back home, she opened up the app to see what was going on.

Hmmm.

Travis, 34, 6'1, Engineer. So *far, so good!* Has kids. Not a dealbreaker. *Wait, is that a toddler though? Nope. Not trying to entertain baby mama drama.* She swiped left.

Chris, 37, 6', City Planner, No kids. Looking for something casual. *Yeah....I've had enough of that.*

Not jumping into anything fast, but that is giving fuck boy vibes. She swiped left again. *Maybe the third time would be the charm.*

Jace, 39, 5'10, Teacher, No kids. Okay. I guess I can work with this. He's cute. Not fine, but fine alone hasn't gotten me that far. I guess I have to be more open and give it a try. She swiped right. *They matched.*

Well, okay. Here goes nothing!

Chapter 4
Reunited

Danielle and Jace exchanged a few messages back and forth. He didn't have game like Marcus, but that is what had gotten her in trouble before. He was, however, a savvy communicator and good with the banter. After a fun exchange about some shared interests, he eventually asked her out, so here she was. Getting back out there. They decided they would meet up on Thursday evening. He wanted to meet sooner, but she had the Journalists of Color conference in town all week and wouldn't be free until Thursday.

She decided it was time to bring in the group chat to the recent developments. Even Brandy didn't know about her setting up the profile.

Nicole was still trying to convince someone to run an upcoming half marathon with her when Danielle interrupted with, "Girl, you know I only run if I'm being chased! But maybe that's only literally now...."

"..."

"Whatchu talkin' 'bout Willis?!" Jasmine interjected. A fan of 80s TV sitcoms, Jasmine loved using this reference from *Diff'rent Strokes*.

"Well...I have a date next Thursday."

"Wait! I just saw you and you said you were swearing off men. How did we go from zero to a date?! But yay!" Brandy exclaimed.

"Okay, back story. I ended things with Marcus last weekend. Just couldn't do the noncommittal anymore."

"Aw, good for you, boo. You feeling okay about it?" Classic Ananda.

"I am actually! So on a whim, I went up to Brandy's for the Halloween party and at brunch I definitely said I was going to take some time off from the men folk, but then I had a near run in with Marcus."

"Oh really. I hope he realized what he's missing!" Jasmine jumped in.

"For real." Nicole added.

"Yeah...so I was picking up some wine last night at the shop in my neighborhood and whose voice do I overhear? Yup. Marcus. With some Moscato drinking chick."

"Not the Moscato! Ugh. Vom! If he wants a Moscato girl, then definitely not a match. LOL!" Brandy added.

"So wait, did you have to see him..and her? What did she look like?" Nicole asked.

Oh no! Fortunately I was able to pay and leave without a run in. And good thing. I had a long ass day and definitely didn't look cute! But anyway. Got home. Had a few glasses of wine and decided to get on Link."

"Oh damn! Okay girl. Good for you. What pics did you use? You already matched with someone? Inquiring minds WANT. TO. KNOW." You'd think Jasmine was the journalist with all those questions.

"I'll show you. But yeah. I did match with someone. Trying to be more open, so we'll see. He's a bit older and shorter than I would have wanted, but tall, younger, and fine ain't done shit for me, so worth a shot! Plus. We've had some good text exchanges so we'll see!"

"Being open is a good thing! I mean, think about me and Kai. We probably wouldn't have

met online if I went based on my previous criteria," Ananda added.

"Good point, good point. Anyway...I'll keep y'all posted!"

The girlfriends exchanged a few more texts before it got quiet and they all went about their respective Saturday business. Danielle took another few peeks at the app and swiped on a few more guys before closing down for the day. While things with Jace had promise, mama ain't raise no fool! She was keeping her options open.

The rest of her weekend was uneventful and Danielle had an early bedtime on Sunday night because she knew she had a busy week ahead at her conference. Between all day sessions, dinners, drinks, and more, she needed all the rest she could get.

The next morning, Danielle was at the conference center bright and early. She had just filled up a coffee and was walking to retrieve her badge when she heard, "Danielle!" She looked around the large open space to see who was calling her name.

"Danielle! Hey!" She saw a vaguely familiar face walking toward her with a smile. She put it together by the time he approached.

"Oh hey...Andrew. Nice to see you again." In their Uber adventure, it didn't come up that Andrew would be attending the conference. Honestly, Danielle didn't think to ask. Andrew looked more white-presenting, but apparently, as she would learn later, is actually white and, proudly, Puerto Rican.

"Yeah. Great to see you, too. What sessions are you hitting up this morning?"

"Um..." she looked down at her schedule. "Representation in Storytelling and Women in Broadcast Media. What about you?"

"Engaging Diverse Communities in Reporting and Designing Your Editorial Strategy. You have plans for lunch? Would be great to catch up."

"Nope. Not booked until dinner. And sounds good."

"Cool. Here's my number. Just text me when you are headed to the ballroom." They exchanged numbers and parted ways.

Danielle had a productive morning of sessions before lunch. She made her plate in the buffet line, found a seat in the ballroom, and then sent a text to Andrew. He found her a few minutes later and sat down.

During the first few minutes of their conversation, she got to know more about Andrew. He definitely wasn't what she assumed from when she first met him. Yet another reminder that she needed to be open with and about people. They actually had a lot in common. He also came from humble beginnings. He grew up with a single mom in the Bronx after his dad passed away, attended public schools, and was inspired to be a journalist after a teacher noticed his penchant for writing. Now that she thought about it, was he actually kind of...cute? Before she had a chance to fully process if she was now a little into him, she was snapped back into reality when she heard him use the g-word.

Girlfriend.

Well, where was she on Halloween night? Before she could ask, Andrew answered and mentioned she had a pre-planned girls trip. He had wanted to do Clark Kent and Lois Lane, but had to be the black-eyed pea instead. They had just started talking about their morning sessions when a figure approached the table.

The face was familiar. Danielle had seen him on and off over the years at conferences and happy hours and they'd exchanged brief pleas-antries, but she couldn't recall his name.

"Hey man, what's up?" Andrew said as he greeted the guy. " Danielle, this is..."

Chapter 5
Blake

"Blake." The man interrupted and offered his hand to Danielle. "Blake Tanner."

Blake. That was it. She wasn't always great with names, so it didn't surprise her that it didn't stick, but she should have remembered Tanner since it was the last name of her favorite artist, Henry Ossawa Tanner. But maybe she'd been so hung up on Marcus that she wasn't ever noticing anyone else around her.

Blake sat down with his plate. Danielle learned that he and Andrew had become friends through the conference scene over the years. Blake was an editor at a sports magazine and lived in Baltimore, not too far from Danielle. Although the similarities stopped there. He grew up a Jack and Jill kid in Virginia and attended a prestigious boarding school in D.C. before going to Morehouse. Danielle had just learned what Jack and Jill was last year through a quick Google search when someone mentioned it at a party. She also learned he had an affinity for contemporary art and often took his nephew to galleries around town. He also volunteered with an after school program. Interesting guy. Quite different from most the guys she grew up with, hung out with, or dated.

Before too long, it was time to get to their next sessions. They said their farewells and Danielle went about the rest of her day packed with conference sessions and connecting with colleagues. She also exchanged a couple texts with Jace in anticipation of their Thursday date and matched with a few other guys on Link.

Her subsequent conference days were rather uneventful. She'd say a quick hello to Andrew and Blake when she saw them, but didn't get a chance to really connect with them again until Wednesday. During the afternoon coffee hour, they invited Danielle out with them later. She had dinner plans with a colleague, but said she would meet up with them at a bar afterward. Guess they wanted to do it up big on the last night of the conference!

Hours later, Danielle was pulling open the door to a retro-style dive bar complete with pool tables, arcade games, and darts. 'I Will Survive' emitted from a jukebox. She felt over-dressed for the location, but figured she would make an appearance then take herself home to get out of this dress, tights, and boots. She spotted Andrew and Blake at the far end of the bar and walked up.

"Danielle! Hey!" Andrew greeted her with a big hug. He clearly had had a few beers already.

Blake also greeted her with a hug. "Hey. How ya doin'?" he asked. She noticed he smelled really good.

"Good, good," she replied as she stepped back. She thought maybe she noticed Blake eyeing her just a bit, but she'd already had a healthy pour of wine at dinner so maybe she was just a bit buzzed.

"Beer?" Andrew pulled a beer out of a bucket in front of the guys and offered it to Danielle.

"Sure!" she said, taking the bottle and taking a sip.

"Damn. How many games did you play?" she asked with a chuckle as she pointed her bottle toward the stash of yellow tickets the guys had earned from the arcade games.

"That's all Drew. Who knew he was a Pac Man prodigy?!" Blake added.

"Oh okay. None for you?"

"I guess I added a few."

Before Blake could continue sharing about his game prowess, he heard the intro notes to a song Danielle didn't immediately recognize and he started singing along passionately.

"In my eyes...Indisposed...in disguises no one knows..." Blake belted out the opening line of 'Black Hole Sun' by Soundgarden, which Danielle eventually gathered. She only knew it from what she affectionately called one of Brandy's "white girl playlists." As Brandy told her, "you can take the girl out of the suburbs, but not the suburbs out of the girl." As he continued to sing along, Danielle couldn't help but wonder if he dated Black girls or not. I mean, she was learning to be open to people not being what they seem, but she wasn't sure.

"Yo! I'm usually much more of a hip hop head, but that one brings back memories from my private school days."

"Gotcha. Surprisingly, I know this one too." She gave her head a little shake and laughed.

"For real. Okay. Dope!"

"Yeah. My best friend grew up in the suburbs with a lot of white folks and went through an alternative phase. I think that's what you call it. I don't know. I grew up on classic soul, R&B, and hip hop, but we had different childhoods!" She paused for a sip of her drink. "But my horizons have expanded thanks to, B. Just don't let her play Spotify on random! It's a literal trip."

"Where did you grow up?"

"Not too far from here."

"So wait. Then, how did you meet your alternative music loving best friend?"

"College. We were randomly assigned as roommates. Actually. She is how I met Andrew. Sort of. Did he tell you the story about Halloween night?"

"That night!" Andrew interjected. "I didn't think we were ever gonna make it off that bridge!"

As Andrew proceeded to tell the story, Danielle observed Blake a little more closely. He was really handsome. Smooth, chocolate skin. A well-groomed beard he stroked when intensely engaged in conversation. Perfectly straight white teeth. She snapped back into the conversation when she heard Blake say, "We're up!"

They relocated to a high top table near the pool table. Blake started setting up for a round of pool while Andrew straggled behind refreshing their bucket of beers.

"You play?" Blake asked.

"Nope. Tried a few times, but never got the hang of it."

"Guess you needed a better teacher," he responded with a wink.

Is he flirting? She felt a little flushed. No. *My flirt radar is off. I mean, I thought Andrew was flirting before and he has a whole ass girlfriend. But if he is flirting, should I play along? I mean, why not? He's cute. It could be fun. Even though* she was excited about this date tomorrow with Jace, she wasn't committed to anyone.

"You volunteering for the job?" she asked.

"I'm happy to offer my services." He held the pool cue in one hand and took a swig of his beer with the other, never breaking eye contact. "How 'bout this? Watch this round with me and Drew. Then, we'll rack again and I'll show ya."

"Okay...deal. What do I get if I win?"

"Ohhhh okay. I see you. You the wagering type. You think you're gonna get lucky. How 'bout..."

Just then Andrew walked back up with the beers. "What I miss?"

The guys began their pool game while Danielle escaped to the bathroom. She needed to update the girls. Inside the safety of the stall she opened up her phone and went to start the text when she noticed a few texts from Jace. She felt an unfamiliar nagging in her belly. This was just...different. Being interested in two guys. At the same time. That was more Nicole's wheelhouse. She'd barely ever been interested in more than one at a time. She definitely needed the group chat now. This was not her comfort zone at all.

"How y'all do that thing when you are interested in more than one dude at once? How do you manage it all?" she quickly typed out. She saw three dots appear immediately from Brandy. Thursday night was Jalen's basketball league so she knew B was at home drinking wine and binge watching her solo shows.

"What I miss now?! Get it, get it! Call me!" Brandy replied.

"Can't. At the bar with the newest one. Will call you tomorrow though. But for real though. This is such foreign territory."

"Embrace it, boo! Have fun! Let them wine and dine you. You deserve it!" Nicole added.

"Get to know them both. You don't have to decide today." Ananda added.

"Can we at least have something to call them both?" Brandy added. She knew guys didn't get real names until they were official.

"Let's call tonight's guy Beard and the other one Teacher."

"Good luck. Keep us posted!" Nicole replied.

Chapter 6
Lessons

Danielle shot off a quick text to Jace. She'd get to see what the vibe was with him tomorrow, but for now, she was going to see what was happening back out there with Blake. She went back out where the guys were continuing to play pool. She sipped on the beer and observed the basics of the game. Well that and Blake's butt as he leaned over the pool table.

A few moments later, Andrew's phone rang. It was his girlfriend.

"Be right back," he stated as he passed his pool cue to Danielle and walked toward the front door of the bar.

"Well. Guess your lesson is starting early," Blake stated. Danielle placed her beer down on the table. Blake started explaining a few basics of the game, including how to make a shot. He stepped behind her to help guide her. "Do you mind?" he inquired.

"No. Not at all," she replied.

He placed his body against and his hand on top of hers, helping her find the rhythm of the stroke of the cue. She couldn't help but wonder about the rhythm of some other kinds of strokes. They practiced a few other angles before he set her free to try on her own. She hit the ball successfully into the pocket. He pulled her into an embrace to celebrate!

"See?! I told you. You just needed the right teacher."

"Indeed I did."

They pulled apart just as Andrew came back. Danielle handed him back the pool cue and he and Blake continued to play, only pausing the game to sing and dance along to 'Poison' for a minute. This man was full of surprises. They played another round of pool and a couple of arcade games, drank a few more beers, and sang and danced along to some other classics. Before long, they decided to depart. It was getting late and they all had the last day of the conference tomorrow.

Danielle wanted to find a way to scheme into the Uber with Blake, but he was heading in a different direction. Andrew was headed back to the hotel, which was in the direction of her place so it made more sense to ride with him. She didn't want to look thirsty, especially in front of Andrew, so she decided to play it cool and just figured she'd see him at the conference tomorrow. She had hoped he might have asked for her number, but he hadn't. *Sigh...maybe he was just being friendly, or even flirty, but not actually interested.* They said their goodbyes and there she was back in an Uber with Andrew.

"Back to where we started, huh?" Andrew stated.

"For real. The Universe is funny like that."

"You have a good night?" he asked. I'm glad you made it out."

"Yeah. It was a good time. Thanks for the invite."

"Oh, of course. It was all Blake's idea," he replied as rested his head on the window, his eyes heavy.

"I see." Danielle mumbled. Meanwhile, she wanted to ask a thousand and one questions.

What did he mean it was Blake's idea? If it was his idea, why didn't he ask for my number? Just like the number of licks to the center of a Tootsie pop, the world may never know. *Maybe it was best to stay friends. After all, they were in the same industry. Maybe that would get messy. Yeah. That would be for the best.*

***

The next morning, Danielle drug herself out of bed.

Oof. She was exhausted.

She was glad it was only a half day of sessions. She'd have time for a nap before her date with Jace. Yes, Jace. She decided to focus her energy back that way. She looked back at their text messages from the night before. A little sparse, but she had mentioned she was busy with the conference. She sent him a quick text saying she was excited for later and then headed out for the day.

In the hubbub of the day, Danielle didn't end up seeing Andrew or Blake during the morning sessions. She figured she would catch up over lunch. Since she didn't have Blake's number, she sent Andrew a text to see if they could meet up. A few minutes later she got a reply.

"Hey. Sorry to miss you, Danielle! Headed back to the city. Vanessa has tickets for a show tonight. Great seeing you again! Let me know when you are back for a visit!"

Damn. Now she had no way of connecting with Blake and seeing if, indeed, anything was still there between them in the light of day. *Must be a sign.*

She went home after the sessions and managed to sneak in a nap. She attempted to put Blake out of her mind, but as she floated into sleep, she couldn't help having flashbacks to the feeling of his warmth and the musky, spicy scent of his cologne.

Chapter 7
Surprise!

A couple of hours later, Danielle was pulling open the door of the bar where she was meeting Jace for happy hour. She spotted him seated on a couch on the opposite side of the bar. He was in conversation with a couple on the couch across from him. When she walked over to where they were seated, Jace stood and awkwardly greeted her with a kiss on the forehead and offered to take her coat.

Okay. That was a little odd. Well, at least he's cuter than his pictures.

She sat down and he handed her the drink menu. As she scanned the list of drinks, the tipsy woman seated on the couch across from them chimed in. "Glad you finally made it. Thought you were going to leave this guy here stranded!"

What? We were always meeting at 6:30. It's 6:30. Weird.

She looked up and added "Oh I'm right on time!" with her fake customer service smile and "I will cut a bitch" eyes. She looked back down at the menu. Jace continued to talk to the couple. Apparently, he had arrived early and struck up a conversation with them. They must have assumed, or he didn't correct them, that I was late for this date.

The cocktail waitress cut some of the tension in the air when she approached and asked for Danielle's drink choice. "I'll just do a rum and pineapple, please."

"Really?" Jace asked. "You really should try one of the cocktails. They're known for them here."

"I'm good with what I ordered for now," she replied. She *really* didn't like being told what she should do, but she chalked it up to Jace being nervous or awkward or something. She decided to redirect the conversation and get to know him a little better. "How was your day?"

"Ah. Not too bad. Glad tomorrow is Friday. My 10th grade class is a bunch of assholes." He took a big sip of his drink.

"I mean, I guess that comes with the age group, right? My cousin teaches high school, too, and they drive her crazy, but she really loves them."

"Hmm," he replied.

Gratefully, Danielle's drink arrived at that moment. She took a sip. "So, have you lived in Baltimore long?"

"Yeah. I've been here about 10 years now."

"Gotcha. About the same for me, too," she volunteered.

"Cool cool." He took another large sip of his drink then asked, "So, let's cut to the chase here. Why are you still single, Danielle?"

Is he serious? Who asks that?

"Umm, well. I haven't met the right person yet."

"That's what they all say. What's the real deal? Can't get over an ex? Impossible standards?"

Sure, she had dealt with some emotional unavailability, but that was too vulnerable of a thing to share with a guy who tried to tell her what to order and didn't know how to ask questions.

"None of the above," she said flatly, yet firmly. She took another sip of her drink.

"Okay, time will tell," he said, and moved his arm behind her on the couch. She knew at that moment, the only thing time would tell is how much longer she would be staying on this lackluster date. Danielle got quiet and sipped her drink. Quiet was better than her telling him the hell off. She could get past the fact that he wasn't her physical type, per se, but not over his behavior and character.

"Excuse me. I'll be right back," Danielle stated after finishing her drink. She knew better than to leave a drink unattended.

She walked through the bar to the bathroom. Here she was again, in a bathroom, texting her group chat letting them know this date was a dud to which they responded with encouraging words about being proud of her for getting back out there. She gave herself a look in the bathroom mirror. If the date was going well, she would have swiped on some more lipstick and sprayed another sprtiz of perfume, but she no longer cared and was ready to make her departure.

As she approached the seat and planned to say her goodbye, she noticed the waitress coming back over with a drink refill. *Dammit! I thought I was in the clear.*

For better or worse, even though Danielle was a confident, assertive woman who normally didn't mind speaking her mind, given her inexperience with actual relationships, she sometimes struggled with when to say enough. Also, years of conditioning about being good and nice were hard to break. She said thank you and started working on her second drink. Maybe it would make this time more palatable.

It didn't.

Jace continued to invite the couple across the couch into their conversations and talk about himself more than asking questions. Danielle had reached her limit. She would be happier at home on her couch.

"I've had a long day. I'm thinking about heading out," Danielle shared.

"Already?! We were just getting to know each other. You don't want to grab some food?" he asked obliviously.

"Oh no, thanks. I'm okay."

"You're going to miss out on the best burger in the city, but whatever. I'll walk you out at least." He left some cash on the table for the waitress.

They left the bar and emerged onto the city sidewalk. It was brisk in the air and Jace attempted to put his arm around Danielle. She shrunk away from his touch and said, "I'm okay." She pulled out her phone to grab an Uber. When she looked back up from the phone she did a double take.

No. It couldn't be. And no! Not me with this guy!

Chapter 8
Finally

Danielle saw two male figures heading her direction down the block and it was indeed Andrew and Blake.

How? Her brain couldn't compute fast enough, but she did have enough wherewithal to step further away from Jace. *What would Blake think?*

"Andrew? Blake? Hey!" she moved toward them to go give them a hug and for some damn reason, Jace was behind her like a puppy dog. Was he threatened by them? She wasn't even into him for that to be a reasonable response.

"D!" Andrew said excitedly. "Dude. I was on my way back to the city and there was a train derailment so I'm not getting out of here until tomorrow, so Blake came through in the clutch." Now it made sense. And indeed, she wasn't dreaming.

"Hey Danielle," Blake said evenly.

"Hey," she replied, wondering what was going through his head. In this moment, she realized just how much she liked him and hoped this wouldn't be a deterrent.

"Come hang with us!" Andrew said, putting his arm around her.

"I think she's tired," Jace interjected.

Danielle, sick of his shit, spoke up and said, "I think *she* can speak for herself. Have a good night." Jace looked dejected and turned to walk away. Not without muttering "bitch..." under his breath.

"I strongly suggest you keep walking and keep your mouth shut about the lady," Blake said, sternly, looking Jace directly in the eye. Jace continued walking.

Danielle had to admit that Blake stepping up for her was pretty hot. But now what? Her Uber was pulling up. Did she risk looking silly and say something? Did she just go home and wonder what if? There was no guarantee she'd just run into Blake again and they still hadn't exchanged phone numbers.

Dammit! She was so flustered that she just quickly and awkwardly said, "Thanks, guys. Gotta run." She got in the Uber and it drove in the direction of her home.

Seriously, Danielle? Old habits die hard, she decided, as she reverted back to her pattern of not being vulnerable. But what now?

She pulled out her phone.

"Ugh. I'm a fucking idiot, y'all! Can't even get into all the details, but my date with Teacher was awful. Then, I randomly ran into Beard outside the bar, and here I am in the Uber on the way home. What is wrong with me?"

"No! Girl, go get your man! #TeamBeard!" Jasmine was the first to respond.

"For real?! Did you ever get his number, D?" Nicole asked.

"No..." Danielle reluctantly responded. "So now what?"

"He's friends with Andrew, right? Tell him to give you the digits!" Brandy exclaimed.

"Yeah, I could. But would that be doing the most?" Danielle wondered.

"No!" Jasmine added.

"We'll see. I will let y'all know. Thanks!"

In true BFF fashion, Brandy sent a separate text to Danielle. "D. I've known you for over a decade and I've never heard you like this. Seems like you have some serious feels for him. Maybe it's worth doing the scary thing," Brandy responded.

"Yeah. Maybe." She put her phone down on her lap and looked out the window for a few blocks. *Maybe I will ask Andrew for his number?*

When she looked down, she realized that somehow she had a missed call and a voicemail from a number not saved in her phone. *Well, how did that happen?* She wondered as she put in her earbuds and pressed the play button. Her jaw dropped as she listened.

"Danielle, it's Blake. Got your number from Drew. Hope you don't mind. Listen, I should have said something back at the bar before you got in the Uber. I guess I was caught off guard...can you call me back? I've wanted to ask you out since I saw you the first day of the conference. And it took seeing you with someone else for me to realize I didn't want to miss my chance."

"Hey. I need to change the address in the app, but can you turn around? I need to go back where I was before?" she quickly told the driver. She changed the address back to the bar. Then she called the number back. He picked up!

"Blake, it's me!"

"Danielle, where are you? I'm coming to meet you."

"Stay by the bar. I"m on my way!"

Minutes later, Danielle pulled back up in front of the bar where Blake was standing. She couldn't get out of the car fast enough and into the arms that he opened to welcome her in.

Chapter 9
Home

A few weeks later, Danielle was back in New York for a long weekend. At Brandy's recommendation, she and Blake had a romantic stay in Bliss Bay that happened to coincide with the harvest festival. They had a fabulous time soaking in the hot tub, drinking mulled wine, and staring at the stars by the bonfire.

They returned refreshed to Brooklyn on Saturday for massages at their hotel and an evening at the Brooklyn Museum with Brandy and Jalen. On Sunday, she found herself brunching with Brandy and Gabby, catching them up on the whirlwind romance with "Beard," whose actual name she had finally revealed to her friends once things were official.

"Look at you glowing!" Gabby exclaimed. "I knew something like this was going to happen. Didn't I tell you?!"

The waitress placed three mimosas in front of the women. Brandy made them do a Boomerang before she said, "Cheers! Okay now, D. All the deets! Spare nothing!"

"Well, it started after that last night of the conference…"

Danielle started as she recounted how that night, after she found herself in Blake's embrace, they ended up back at his place, with Andrew in tow. Andrew was passed out on the couch while they sat at Blake's kitchen table talking for hours. There she learned how he had always had his eye on her, but could tell by her energy she was "occupied" so let it go. But he figured it was the Universe's doing when their orbit's intersected at the conference. When they finally decided to crash, he was the perfect gentleman offering her some spare clothes and the bed to herself. She obliged. She was into him, but needed a bit more time before things got more physical. She appreciated that he respected that.

"But that all changed this weekend…" Danielle said slyly.

"Oooh!" Gabby replied. "We're going to need more drinks for this!" She made eye contact with the waitress who came over and refreshed their mimosas.

"Shut. The. Front. Door." Brandy eyes enlarged with excitement. She picked up her knife and pretended it was a microphone. She activated her "radio voice."

"We are live from Sunday brunch at Pastis where Danielle is about to disclose the dirty details of her evening escapades with Blake. Danielle?" She pointed the knife toward Danielle.

"Thank you, Brandy," she said, speaking into the "mic." She took a large gulp of her mimosa. "So it must have been something about that Bliss Bay air...between that and the wine...we couldn't keep our hands off each other. It was just...delicious. Slow. Sweet."

"Yeahhhhhh!" Gabby interjected.

"But the real spicy part happened last night. After we left you all, we decided to do a nightcap at the hotel. We started out in the hotel bar, which if you haven't tried yet, is super dope. Dark, moody. Well, we were about to be those people where folks would say 'get a room,' but, wait. We had a room. So needless to say, we took our drinks back up there."

"And then..." Brandy leaned in.

"And then, Blake said he had a surprise for me and that I should get comfortable and relax. So I did. I sat in that amazing leather chair by the window, sipped on my drink and really took it all in. The city views, the vibe..." She took another sip of mimosa. "A few minutes later, I heard him call me in to the bathroom where he had set up that amazing tub with...freaking rose petals! Like how and when did he sneak those in to set this up I don't know, but it was like a damn dream!"

"Well played," Gabby added as she slow clapped for Blake. "Well. Played."

"So I knew it was going to be on at that moment. And that buzz was feeling good. So I started to slowly pull down the straps of my dress. Then this fool is gonna be like 'Hold on, a minute!'"

"What? Bless his heart!" Gabby added.

"I was about to have questions, but he was just quickly grabbing his phone to put on some music. So he put on some Leon Bridges and then told me he was ready. So I proceeded to undress and ever so slowly ease my way into the tub."

"Yassss!" Brandy said, excitedly busting out into a little body roll.

"I told him I couldn't be in there all alone. So he obliged. He got undressed and joined me in there."

Gabby's jaw had dropped. "Go on, go on."

"That part was sweet. Well, that's how it started. For a hot second. He held me, kissed my neck, and then, it got a little hotter." Danielle's audience was captive. They paused only for the waitress to place their plates of eggs, pancakes, bacon, and french fries in front of them.

Danielle continued. "Well, then we knew we had to change location after making a bit of a mess with the water..."

"Splish splash!" Brandy exclaimed. Danielle chuckled.

"So he grabs me by the hand and leads me to the bed and lays me down ever so gently. Kisses me softly all over my body. And I mean...All. Over. Everything was just warm and slow. It was almost like an out of body experience except my body felt it all. After we finished, he just held me until I fell asleep. No rush to leave or pull away to his own space. It was divine!"

"Awwww. I love it!" Gabby chimed in.

"Oh I'm not finished though." Danielle added with a sly smile.

"There's more?!" Brandy shrieked. She then realized she was drawing a little too much attention to them, so she whispered, "There's more?"

"Yes honey. Let's just say it went from warm to hot! That's why I was a few minutes late this morning."

"I knew it!" Brandy exclaimed.

"Girl. I don't know what came over me, but something about him makes me feel just so comfortable and uninhibited. It was like I felt some sort of primal connection to him." She dropped her voice to a bit more of a whisper. "So, I decided to give him a special wake up call. If you know what I mean."

"Really..."Gabby said, intrigued.

"Oh yeah. I mean, I could *feel* that he was *up* and so, you know." Danielle gave the gist of what happened, but kept the super salacious details of how she woke Blake up with a trail of kisses down his abdomen and on his inner thighs before taking him into her mouth. She continued with the parts she would share. "So we took a little time out, and then it was his turn." She made a fanning motion with her hand.

"Ahh. Nothing like hot, sober, Sunday morning sex!" Brandy said wistfully. Not without a few eyes from the family at the table next to them. She offered a forced smile and then turned back to the girls. "They should know what Sunday brunch talk is all about! Keep going, D!"

"So...we ended up on that large leather chair in the room. You know the one next to those epic, large windows with the city view. Let's just say, I will always look at that skyline with such fond memories..."

"Save a horse, ride a cowboy! Ha!" Brandy got a kick out of herself and giggled.

"Something like that!" Danielle replied. "So after all that, we needed to shower and well, then that led to even more fun and now here I am!" she concluded.

She didn't mind sharing, but wasn't always the most comfortable with sharing the most explicit details even though she very much enjoyed doing the explicit things. Like how he teased her with the various water pressures from the detachable shower head before entering her. How he followed her guidance to move in and out slowly, as he had her pressed up against the shower wall, engulfed in steam, letting the tension build before she eked out a breathy "faster!" How she let out a shriek unlike any she'd ever heard come out of her mouth while digging her nails into his back. How he nibbled her neck as he found his own release. How she wondered if the bathroom walls were sound-proof. If not, sorry neighbors!

"Well, this calls for another toast!" Gabby said as she raised her glass.

"Agreed!" Brandy added. "Don't forget the eye contact though. Because you know...seven years of bad sex. Although...the way your man put it down, I'm not sure if it would ever be bad, D. But no chances!"

"Thanks, y'all! Cheers!" Danielle replied. The three women clinked their glasses together in a toast.

An hour or so later, the women found themselves outside of the restaurant. Blake had come to retrieve Danielle for them to head back to Baltimore. Danielle gave Brandy and Gabby big hugs as she said goodbye. Then, she got into the back seat of the cab that would take them to the train station. Blake followed in behind. As the cab drove off, he clasped her hand with his.

"Hey," he said, looking at her.

"Hey back," she said. Then, she rested her head on his shoulder. They were headed back to Baltimore, but as far as Danielle was considered, she was already home.

Chapter 10
Epilogue

Gabby

"Hi. Sorry I'm late..." Gabby said as she hugged her cousin, Brandy, who was already seated at their usual happy hour table. Exasperated, she plopped into her seat and then placed her Bergdorf bag on the chair next to her.

"Ooh! What did you get?!" Brandy asked, excitedly. "Show me!"

"Well, I needed a little pick me up and so..." Gabby reached into the bag and pulled out the sleek black box. She opened the lid. "I got these!" She revealed the gorgeous, gold, 4-inch heels adorned with crystals. They were equal parts fierce and fabulous.

"Wow! Those are amazing! But wait...what happened that you needed a Level 10 pick me up?" Brandy stated, with a hint of worry. Over the years, the two women had developed their own cousin speak. Level 10 was reserved for the most extravagant of purchases to deal with the most epic life events.

"Let me get some bubbly in me before we go there."

"Well look at Gawd!" Brandy joked, with a little chuckle. At just that moment, their server brought over their bucket of bubbly on ice and poured two fresh glasses.

Gabby didn't wait to toast. She drained her first glass and then poured herself some more. Then took another sip.

"Okay...so the past 48 hours have been a bit of a cluster...and I'm not sure what I'm going to do," Gabby choked, tears brimming in her eyes.

"Gab! What happened?!" Brandy exclaimed. She rubbed her cousin's forearm and gave her hand a squeeze.

"Well, Dev and I broke up."

Brandy's eyes got as big as saucers. "Seriously..." she replied, sadly, empathetically, in almost a whisper.

"Yeah. That happened." She sipped some more of her bubbly. "I just couldn't do it anymore, B. It's been five. Effing. Years. And he still wouldn't move in together. I mean, damn. I know my biological clock isn't ticking because I don't want babies, but I am ready for the next level. And get this. To make it worse. This dude was planning to just go off to Boston for the summer. Never mentioned it to me."

"Wait, what? Why?" Brandy asked, incredulously.

"He got some fellowship. Like, great for him professionally, but there was no conversation. And I just knew. He wasn't trying to build a future with me. He likes me. Loves me even. But I want a real partnership and he just can't give that to me." She dabbed her eyes with a napkin. What she wasn't ready to admit, to her cousin or anyone else, was that she'd had a nagging feeling that things might end up this way.

Aww. I'm sorry."

"Thanks. So, that was *my* Sunday. And even though it was my choice, it still sucks. Here I am. At 39. Starting over again..." Gabby eked out, fighting back the floodgate of tears. "And you know I was going through it because I took a day off work! And I never do that." Gabby sighed deeply while Brandy let her speak and just listened.

On the inside, Brandy both wanted to reassure her cousin that she was a catch and everything would be okay and also that she was ready to fuck up Dev's life, if needed be, but she held her tongue and just held space. She knew that was the best thing she could do thanks to her dear friend, Ananda, a practicing therapist.

Gabby continued. "So yeah. I just felt like I needed some time to process and couldn't bear even discussing it. I barely pulled myself out of bed yesterday. But I did. Took myself to brunch. They probably thought I was bat shit crazy because I had sunglasses on the whole time..." She sipped some more of her drink. Then, I got a last minute massage , ent home ,and finally called Amaya." Amaya was Gabby's best friend. "Then I ordered takeout, drank copious amounts of bourbon, and cried myself to sleep. So yeah...I left work early today and...here we are!" She exclaimed, motioning toward her shoes.

"G...I'm so sorry. That's a lot," Brandy empathized.

"Yeah...so, we'll see. Maybe I just need a break from reality or to move or something. It's like every street I walk down has a damn memory attached to it..."

"Ugh. The absolute worst. Well, it's not moving, but...there is room in our house in Bliss Bay this summer! Could be a good distraction. I mean, it's more a sandals than stilettos vibe so you won't be able to wear those beauties," Brandy nodded toward the box of heels. "But...maybe it's just the kind of break your heart needs."

Gabby paused. Summer was quickly approaching and she didn't have any other plans. Well, not anymore. She and Dev had talked about booking a trip later that summer, but never got around to booking. *Well, why the hell not?*

"Okay. Let's do it!"

Thank You

Thank you for reading *Danielle: A Bliss Bay Romance!* If you enjoyed this book, I would be grateful if you could leave a review. Reviews help boost book sales. As an indie author, they are especially helpful!

Thank you!

Kayla

Bliss Bay Series

Want more from Bliss Bay? Buy book 1, *Brandy*, and book 3, *Gabby*. Plus other fun bonus content at Give them Romance https://www.give themromance.com/

About the Author

Kayla Love has been writing since she could put a pen in her hand. While she's mostly written non-fiction, she's excited to venture into the Bliss Bay series as her first works of fiction. Her goal is to write compelling, fun, and real romance stories that reflect the diverse experiences of Black women like herself and the other the women of color in her world. Many of her characters and storylines are inspired by her time living in New York, including numerous summers at the beach.

Like her character, Brandy, Kayla was born and bred in New Jersey, loves spending time at the beach, eating bacon, and drinking black coffee and Cabernet Franc. A founding Corner of Press author, Kayla now resides in California.